A WONDERFUL YEAR

NICK BRUEL

YAWN

A NEAL PORTER BOOK
ROARING BROOK PRESS
New York

In memory of Louise Nyssens Bruel

PART ONE
Winter Wear

IT'S SNOWING!
IT'S SNOWING!
IT'S SNOWING!
IT'S...

"It's cold outside! You'd better wear your boots," said her mother.

"You'd better wear your earmuffs," said her father.

"You'd better wear your snowpants," said the dog.

"You'd better wear your scarf," said the cat.

"You'd better wear your gloves," said Louise.

"You'd better wear your sweater," said the tree.

"You'd better wear your hat," said the refrigerator.

"You'd better wear your coat," said the can of beans.

"Thanks," said the girl.

And off she went.

PART TWO
Spring Splendor

Behold a Fairy Princess!
A Princess!
A Princess!
Behold a Fairy Princess,
A fair maiden she!

Behold a yellow daffodil!
A daffodil!
A daffodil!
Behold a yellow daffodil,
As pretty as can be!

Behold a spotted butterfly!
A butterfly!
A butterfly!
Behold a spotted butterfly,
That flies in front of me!

Behold a handsome puppy dog!
A puppy dog!
A puppy dog!
Behold a handsome puppy dog,
A loyal dog is he!

Behold a knight in armor!
In armor!
In armor!
Behold a knight in armor,
A warrior is he!

We are a happy duo!
A duo!
A duo!
We are a happy duo,
A jolly pair are we!

Go...

AWAY.

Zzzzz

sigh
Behold a sleeping DRAGON!
A dragon!
A dragon!
Behold a sleeping dragon,
With treasure at his feet!

Shhhhh...
We must be very quiet.
So quiet.
So quiet.
We must be very quiet
To steal the treasure that he keeps!

We took his magic rubies!
His rubies!
His rubies!
We took his magic rubies!
And now we have to FLEEEEE!

zZZZz

PART THREE
Summer Sidewalks

"GOSH! It sure is hot today!"

said Louise.

"I know,"

said the girl.

"GADZOOKS!"
said Louise.

"Fortunately,
I know just what
to do!"

SLURRRP!

SPLORT

"She'll cool down in the freezer!"

"And now to watch a little TV while I wait!"

"GADZOOKS!"
said Louise.

"Fortunately, I know just what to do!"

PART FOUR
Fall Foliage

Once there was a tree who asked the question, "What are you reading?"

"A book of stories about a girl and all of the wonderful things she does throughout the year," the girl replied.

"Are there any trees in it?" wondered the tree.
"I like books about trees."

"Well, yes," said the girl. "There is one tree in it."

"Oh, good!" said the tree. "Is the tree the hero?
I like books where the tree is the hero."

"I wouldn't call him the hero," said the girl.
"But the tree is very brave."

"Oh, I do like books where the tree is brave," said the tree. "What happens?"

"Well, one day all of the tree's leaves begin to change color," said the girl.

"Oh, no!" exclaimed the tree. "They're not green anymore?"

"No," said the girl. "At first they turn a little red . . .

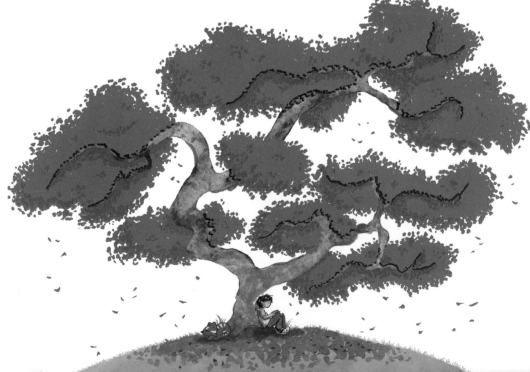

then a little orange . . .

then a little yellow . . .

then a little brown . . .

and then all at once the leaves begin to fall from the tree, showering slowly down onto the ground until there is only one leaf left."

"That sounds awful," said the tree.

"At first that's what the tree thinks," said the girl. "But soon the tree realizes that losing its leaves is like placing a blanket on the ground so its roots can be warm and safe. And the tree knows that after a while it will grow new leaves—leaves that will be just as big and green and lush as the ones it used to have."

"What happens to that last leaf?"
asked the tree.

"I don't know," said the girl. "I haven't read
that far yet."

"I see," said the tree. "May I give you
something before you go?"

"What is it?" asked the girl.

"A bookmark," said the tree.

"Thank you," said the girl.

"It's starting to get cold. You'd better put on a sweater," said the tree with a yawn, just before falling into a deep sleep.

"Thanks," said the girl.

And off she went.

Copyright © 2015 by Nick Bruel · A Neal Porter Book · Published by Roaring Brook Press
Roaring Brook Press is a division of Holtzbrinck Publishing Holdings Limited Partnership
175 Fifth Avenue, New York, New York 10010 · The art for this book was created using ink,
watercolor, gouache, and collage on paper. · mackids.com · All rights reserved

Library of Congress Cataloging-in-Publication Data

Bruel, Nick.
    A wonderful year / Nick Bruel.—First edition.
        pages cm
    "A Neal Porter Book."
    Summary: "A picture book comically following one girl through each of the four seasons"—Provided by publisher.
    ISBN 978-1-59643-611-4 (hardback)
    Seasons—Fiction. 2. Year—Fiction. 3. Humorous stories.] I. Title.
    Z7.B82832Won 2015
    ]—dc23   201400990

Roaring Brook Press books may be purchased for business or promotional use. For information on bulk
purchases please contact Macmillan Corporate and Premium Sales Department at (800) 221-7945 x5442
or by email at specialmarkets@macmillan.com. ·

First edition 2015 · Printed in the United States of America by Phoenix Color Corp. d/b/a Lehigh Phoenix, Rockaway,
New Jersey
10 9 8 7 6 5 4 3 2 1